The
STAR WOLF

DON'T MISS A SINGLE RESCUE!

The Storm Dragon
The Sky Unicorn
The Baby Firebird
The Magic Fox

COMING SOON:

The Sea Pony

The
STAR WOLF

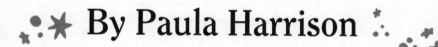

By Paula Harrison

Illustrated by SOPHY WILLIAMS

ALADDIN

New York   London   Toronto   Sydney   New Delhi

For Kiki Rose

ALADDIN

An imprint of Simon & Schuster Children's Publishing Division

1230 Avenue of the Americas, New York, New York 10020

First Aladdin hardcover edition June 2018

Text copyright © 2017 by Paula Harrison

Illustrations copyright © 2017 by Sophy Williams

Originally published in Great Britain in 2017 by Nosy Crow Ltd.

Published by arrangement with Nosy Crow

Also available in an Aladdin paperback edition.

ALADDIN and related logo are registered trademarks of Simon & Schuster, Inc.

For information about special discounts for bulk purchases, please contact Simon & Schuster Special Sales at 1-866-506-1949 or business@simonandschuster.com.

The Simon & Schuster Speakers Bureau can bring authors to your live event. For more information or to book an event contact the Simon & Schuster Speakers Bureau at 1-866-248-3049 or visit our website at www.simonspeakers.com.

Jacket designed by Steve Scott

Interior designed by Nina Simoneaux

The text of this book was set in ITC Clearface.

Manufactured in the United States of America 0518 FFG

2 4 6 8 10 9 7 5 3 1

Library of Congress Control Number 2017954121

ISBN 978-1-4814-7617-1 (hc)

ISBN 978-1-4814-7616-4 (pbk)

ISBN 978-1-4814-7618-8 (eBook)

Chapter One

Berry Picking

Emma stepped out of the front door of her treetop house and breathed in the fresh forest air. The leaves on the branches glowed green and

gold in the sunshine. A squirrel darted along a nearby branch with a nut in its paws.

Emma smiled as she watched the little animal scamper to the ground and start burying the nut in the earth. A cold breeze ruffled her light-brown hair. She picked up her wicker basket and drew her dark-blue cloak tightly around her.

"Bye, Mom! Bye, Dad!" she called. "I'm going to pick some fruit. I'll be back later!"

Holding on to the rail, she crossed a little bridge made from rope and wooden planks. Far

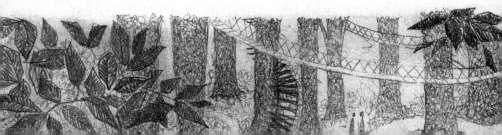

below, the floor of the forest was decorated with the first fallen leaves of autumn.

Emma loved walking through Tangleberry Rise. The whole village was made from wooden tree houses connected by little bridges. Her mom and dad ran a market stall in the middle of the village selling bread, cakes, and pies. Emma liked helping with the stall, although she sometimes felt a little shy in front of all the customers. What she loved most of all was cooking delicious pies and cakes ready for the market.

This morning she was going to gather jem berries to make some lovely pies. At sunset the Lantern Festival would begin. There would be music and dancing and games. Lots of people would want cakes and pies to eat!

Emma skipped across the last bridge and climbed down a little wooden ladder to reach the ground, before following the main path out of the village. Out here, she could hear the sounds of the Whispering Forest more clearly: the squeaks of the mice, the drumming of deer hooves, and the hammering of emerald woodpeckers in the trees. Beneath it all was the whispering of the wind in the leaves that gave the forest its name.

Sometimes, if she was really lucky, Emma heard a golden songbird singing in the treetops. But the most amazing sound of all happened at nightfall, when the star wolves sang.

There were lots of magical animals in the Kingdom of Arramia, like storm dragons, unicorns, firebirds, and cloud bears. The best-known magical  creatures of the Whispering Forest were the star wolves. Hardly anyone had seen them up close, because they were shy animals and lived in the deepest, wildest part of the woods.

Emma had only watched them in the distance, slipping in and out of the trees like silver-gray shadows. Each night their beautiful song drifted over the treetops and lulled her to sleep. Her mom had once explained how their music brought out the evening stars. Without them the night sky would be dark with no starlight at all.

Skipping through the trees, Emma stopped here and there to pick the wild berries that grew by the side of the path. She was heading for the thickest part of the woods, where the red jem berries grew. She found a few strawberries and ate them. They tasted deliciously sweet. There was so much fruit growing here. She knew she'd find plenty to fill up her basket!

She came to a clearing filled with meadow flowers and sat down underneath a huge red-and-white toadstool. Two planets hung together in the sky, one purple and the other green. Giant silverwing butterflies grazed on the flowers, and the chirping of the forest birds filled the air.

Emma started thinking about the Lantern

Festival. She looked forward to it every year. There would be apple bobbing and games like pin the tail on the star wolf. A big bonfire would be lit in the clearing in the middle of the village and a band would play so that everyone could dance.

Emma hurried on, reminding herself that she needed to gather plenty of fruit for the pies. A little farther on she found the thicket of birch trees she was looking for. Jem berry bushes grew all around this part of the woods. Her fingers grew sticky as she picked the berries and put them in her basket. A little mouse scampered out of its hole in the root of a tree and gazed at her, whiskers twitching.

"Here you are!" Emma placed a jem berry on the ground and smiled as the little animal gathered the fruit and scurried back into its hole.

She was about to walk on when she heard a

funny sound. It was a squeaky animal noise, but it was too loud to be a mouse or a rabbit.

Stopping, she listened carefully.

The squeaky sound came again. It went on for a few seconds and then broke off with a sob, as if the animal was crying.

Emma hooked her basket over her arm and pushed her way past some low branches. In the middle of a group of trees was a wooden box buried in a hollow and half covered by earth and leaves. There were thin spaces between the wooden slats and something was moving inside.

As she stepped over a fallen branch, another box snapped shut right next to Emma's foot. She hopped out of the way, her heart thumping. The box had only missed her toes by a whisker!

Stepping more carefully, she crouched down by the first box and looked inside.

A little star wolf with sad black eyes gazed back at her.

Emma stared in surprise. "Hello! How did you get stuck in there?"

A terrible thought popped into her head. Was this an accident or had someone left a trap for the poor animal? Had the box snapped shut on the poor star wolf, just as the other one had almost trapped her foot?

The small star wolf let out a long whimper and scratched against the inside of the box.

"You poor thing!" cried Emma. "No wonder you're so upset."

The creature stopped scratching and howled sadly.

"Here!" Emma took a jem berry out of her basket and put it

through a gap in the wooden slats. "Maybe this will cheer you up!"

The little wolf gulped down the berry and then sniffed Emma's fingers as if hoping for more.

"Now, there must be a way to get you out." Emma put down her basket and knelt beside the box. She pulled at the lid, but it wouldn't open. At last she found a catch in one corner and tugged at it.

The catch sprang open. With a bark of delight, the little wolf jumped out of the box and right into Emma's arms.

She laughed, amazed at how light he felt. "You're so small! You must be a pup."

The little wolf barked again and licked her cheek. Emma ruffled his ears. He was so cute, with deep black eyes and a thick silvery coat. On his forehead was a pale star shape that would gleam when night fell. Every star wolf had this marking and Emma thought it was beautiful. "How could anyone want to trap you? It doesn't make any sense."

The pup sat on his haunches and licked the small pink pads in the middle of his paws.

Emma was about to take another look at the wooden box when she heard voices. Her mind whirled. What if the box belonged to these people? What if they were angry that she'd opened it?

Quickly, Emma picked up the wolf pup and her basket and hid on the other side of the thicket.

A man and a woman dressed in smart brown uniforms came through the trees and stopped next to the boxes.

"We haven't caught a single thing!" said the woman angrily. "No swift hares and no star wolves either. You didn't set the traps properly!"

"That shows you know nothing!" snapped the man. "We did catch something. Look, this one's been opened from the outside." He pointed to the box Emma had undone.

The woman leaned down to look. "Lord Hector's going to be furious. He wants a magical animal caught today and he wants a star wolf most of all."

Emma's heart sank and she clasped the wolf pup tighter. She was right. These people had set the traps on purpose. Someone had told them to do it—someone who wanted to catch magical animals.

Well, they couldn't have this little star wolf. She was going to get him to safety as fast as she could!

Chapter Two

✦ ⁛ ✹

A Lucky Escape

Emma hugged the little star wolf tightly.
She knew her best chance of saving him was
to creep away without the trappers seeing her.

They were still examining the wooden boxes. This was her chance!

"Don't make a sound, okay?" she whispered to the pup.

The little wolf stopped wriggling and pricked up his ears.

Slowly, Emma tiptoed away from the thicket. She trod lightly, careful not to step on any twigs that would crack or leaves that could rustle. The trappers were still talking. To her left she could see the main path leading through the trees.

Emma took another step. Her cloak caught on a bramble and made a loud ripping sound.

She froze.

Her heart thumped. Had the trappers heard the noise?

"Who's there?" yelled the man in the brown uniform. "You'd better come out right now!"

Emma kept absolutely still. The trappers stared around. Then they began searching the under-growth and looking behind trees.

Hurriedly, Emma tugged her cloak free, leaving a scrap of dark-blue cloth stuck on a thorn. Holding the wolf pup tight, she raced toward the main path.

"Hey! Come back!" yelled the woman.

"Stop, thief!" bellowed the man.

Emma ran fast, her heart pounding. The main path was straight ahead, but the man raced round the side of the thicket to cut her off.

Panicking, Emma veered away from the path and into the thickest part of the forest. Crashing through bushes, she kept on running. She didn't dare to look behind her.

Footsteps thudded on the ground. The grown-ups were still chasing and they were getting close.

The star wolf gave a tiny whine. Emma stopped, breathless. Wasn't there anywhere she could hide? Or a tree she could climb? But she couldn't see anything that would help her.

The wolf pup whined louder this time.

"Shh!" Emma stroked him quickly.

"Hey, you!" shouted the man. "Who are you? Turn round and show your face."

"We know you've got our star wolf," the woman snapped. "We can hear it howling."

Emma raced on without turning round. Her

legs were aching and it was hard to catch her breath. She ran across a clearing. It felt scary to be out of the trees, with nothing to hide behind.

A dark cloud floated overhead, blocking out the sunshine.

"Hey! You'd better not—" The man's yelling suddenly stopped.

A strange noise filled the forest—a sort of whooshing sound—coming from the treetops.

Reaching the other side of the clearing, Emma dodged behind a tree. The trappers had stopped chasing her. They were standing still, staring into the air.

A gigantic green creature plummeted from the sky. Emma gasped. It was a dragon with huge webbed wings that stretched almost from one side of the clearing to the other. Landing with a thump that shook the ground, the leathery-skinned creature swung to face the trappers.

A gust of wind made the trees bend and sway.

The dragon let out a long, rumbling growl.

The woman shrieked and ran away. The man bolted after her.

Emma watched them from her hiding place. She was about to slip away into the forest when the dragon turned round and looked straight at her. It didn't growl, just watched her with deep-amber eyes. A curl of smoke drifted from its nostrils.

Something about the creature made Emma feel brave. She stepped out from behind the tree. "You saved me from those horrible trappers," she said. "Thank you!"

The dragon tilted its head to one side, as if wondering what she was saying.

Emma nodded to show she was grateful.

The dragon lifted its wings and gave a deep bow.

Emma smiled and bowed too. Questions raced through her mind. Why was the dragon here? Had it meant to help her? She'd never met a dragon before. No dragons had ever lived in the Whispering Forest. She couldn't help staring at the creature's huge wings and spiny tail.

A fair-haired girl burst into the clearing. She ran right up to the dragon and put a hand on his leathery side. "Windrunner!" she panted. "I didn't think we were meeting here till tonight."

The dragon made a low growly noise, as if it was speaking.

"Really! Where is she?" said the girl.

The dragon nodded its head in Emma's

19

direction, before munching some leaves from the top of a nearby tree.

The girl ran forward. "Hello, I'm Sophy! And this is Windrunner—he's a storm dragon! What's your name? And are you all right? Windrunner told me there were people chasing you."

Emma was too surprised to feel shy. Had this girl really just said that she'd spoken to the dragon? "Um, I'm fine, thank you," she said at last. "My name's Emma. So . . . can you really speak to the dragon?"

"That's right!" Sophy hesitated as if she was deciding whether to share a secret. Then she noticed the wolf pup, half hidden under Emma's cloak. "Wow, is that a star wolf? I've always wanted to meet one." She reached out to tickle the little wolf under the chin.

Emma nodded. "Yes, he's a pup. I found him

stuck in a trap near the birch thicket, so I set him free. That's why those people were chasing me. I just don't understand why they trapped him."

"I might know why." Sophy frowned. "You see, the queen has let her favorite knight, Sir Fitzroy, begin a mission to capture all magical animals. It started when a baby dragon crashed in the castle gardens. Now all magical creatures in the kingdom are in danger."

"That's awful!" The star wolf wriggled so hard in Emma's arms that she had to put him down.

The little pup bounded into the meadow, sniffing at every leaf and flower. Then he gamboled right up to the dragon and licked his leathery foot. Windrunner stopped chewing the leaves and snorted in surprise.

Emma giggled. "He's adorable! But I have to get him back to the wolf pack. He doesn't belong on his own."

"I'd like to help you if you'll let me!" said Sophy eagerly. "And you can tell me about the star wolves and the other forest creatures. I've never been in a forest before today!"

"Of course you can help!" Emma smiled. Somehow she didn't feel shy with Sophy at all. "Welcome to Whispering Forest!"

Chapter Three

Emma's Treetop House

The two girls set off into the woods, waving to the dragon, who flew away to look for the star wolf pack from the air. While they searched among the trees, Emma told Sophy all about the emerald woodpeckers, swift hares, and silver-wing butterflies that lived in the forest. When they got hungry they ate all the fruit that Emma had collected. The wolf pup yawned, so Emma put him into the empty basket, where he curled up on his side and fell fast asleep.

Sophy told Emma all about her life as a maid at the royal castle and how she'd become a secret rescuer of magical animals when a baby dragon crash-landed in the castle garden.

Emma listened to Sophy's tales of meeting other girls who loved magical creatures. She was astonished at how bravely they'd helped the unicorns and firebirds. It all sounded amazing—especially the part about flying around on the back of a dragon!

"So I came here to find out if the magical

animals of the forest are safe," finished Sophy. "I'm lucky to have Windrunner to carry me."

Emma wondered how Sophy could speak to Windrunner the dragon. She was just about to ask when Sophy started telling her about flying over the ocean and what it felt like to glide through a cloud. Sophy chattered on and Emma's eyes grew wider and wider as she listened to it all.

At last they grew tired and returned to the clearing. Emma stroked the wolf pup gently. She loved the softness of his silvery fur and how his ears twitched as he slept. "We should have found the wolf pack by now," she said worriedly. "I hope the trappers didn't scare them away."

"Maybe Windrunner's seen them from the air," said Sophy.

But when the big storm dragon landed in the clearing again, there was no good news.

Emma listened to the dragon's deep growling and wondered how Sophy could possibly understand what it meant.

"Windrunner says he can't help us very much," Sophy told her. "The trees grow so thickly that he can't see anything when he flies over the treetops. The star wolves could be anywhere!"

"And we won't hear them until they begin their song tonight," said Emma thoughtfully.

Sophy hugged the dragon. "Thank you for trying, Windrunner. I'm going to stay and help Emma. I'll meet you here at midday tomorrow."

The dragon bowed to the girls before stretching his massive wings. Wind whooshed around the clearing as he soared into the air. The swirling breeze made the girls' hair flutter.

Emma jumped up. "We can't stay here! Those trappers could be back any minute. Come to my house in Tangleberry Rise and we'll hide the pup there till this evening."

"Great idea!" Sophy beamed. "I can't wait till tonight. I've always dreamed of hearing the star wolves sing!"

They followed the forest path that led to Tangleberry Rise. Emma took the sleeping wolf pup out of the basket and carried him, showing Sophy which berries to collect. "If we pick

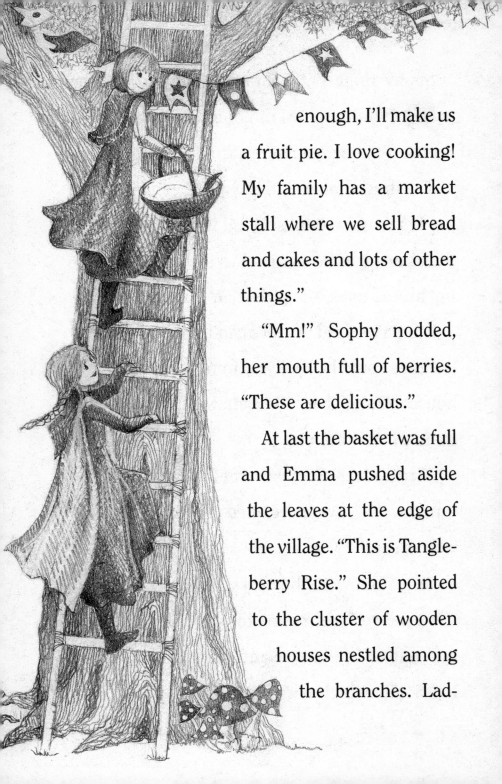

enough, I'll make us a fruit pie. I love cooking! My family has a market stall where we sell bread and cakes and lots of other things."

"Mm!" Sophy nodded, her mouth full of berries. "These are delicious."

At last the basket was full and Emma pushed aside the leaves at the edge of the village. "This is Tangleberry Rise." She pointed to the cluster of wooden houses nestled among the branches. Ladders led up into the treetops and little bridges hung between the tree trunks, making a pathway that linked the village together.

Sophy gasped. "A whole treetop village! You're so lucky to live here!"

Emma pointed to a row of red and blue flags strung between the trees. "Look, they've put up garlands for the Lantern Festival. It's going to be great fun! There'll be games and lots of dancing!" She beckoned Sophy to the nearest ladder. The girls climbed up and crossed the wooden bridges until they reached Emma's house.

"Come in!" Emma opened the door. "My mom and dad will be at the market by now, but they always let me have friends home."

"It's lovely and cozy!" Sophy looked round the sunny room.

Emma shut the door and put the wolf pup

down on a fluffy yellow cushion. The little wolf woke up and yawned, stretching his paws. Then he got down from the sofa to explore.

The wooden walls of the treetop house were decorated with pictures of flowers and rabbits and squirrels. Squashy green sofas with yellow cushions filled the living room. The scent of jam and freshly baked cakes hung in the air.

"It looks like my mom and dad left some treacle pudding for me to eat," Emma called from the kitchen. "Would you like some? And maybe some blackcurrant juice?"

Sophy smiled. "Mm, that sounds yummy! But no, I can't! I mean . . . I would LOVE treacle pudding, but there's something important I've got to tell you first."

Emma's eyes widened. "What is it?"

Sophy took a thread from around her neck.

A small gray stone dangled from the cotton. "You probably wondered how I could talk to Windrunner. This is my Speaking Stone—it lets me talk to all magical animals. It has magic inside—see!" She pulled the stone apart to reveal a little hollow lined with beautiful purple crystals. "This stone works only for me and lets me speak to any magical creature I want."

"Wow!" Emma leaned closer to gaze at the stone. "And it looks so ordinary on the outside!"

The wolf pup bounded up and batted the thread with his paw. Emma scratched his furry head.

Sophy reached into her pocket and drew out a velvety purple bag. "I have some more Speaking Stones in here. Each one will work for the right person, so maybe one of them will work for you!"

Emma's heart jumped. She would love a stone

of her own. Then she could talk to magical animals just like Sophy! "What do I have to do?" she asked.

"Pick one up and hold it in your hands. Then it might change, like mine did." Sophy hesitated. "But . . . don't be too disappointed if it doesn't happen. They don't work for everyone."

Emma's tummy did a little somersault. She really hoped one of the stones worked for her! Taking a deep breath, she picked up the stone she liked best—a round one with smooth sides. The little rock felt cold in her fingers.

She held her breath. Please let it work, she thought. Please, please let the stone change!

The wolf pup crept right up and stared at the stone as if he was wishing for the magic to work too.

Slowly, the rock grew warmer. Emma's hand

tingled as the stone changed from dull gray to bright orange, like a flame springing into life.

It grew hotter and hotter, and then . . . crack! The stone split in half.

"I don't believe it," Emma said breathlessly. "It really worked!"

"I was sure it would!" Sophy grinned widely. "You seemed like the perfect person to have a Speaking Stone. You love animals, don't you?"

Emma blushed. "Of course I do." She turned the two pieces of stone over in her hand. Each one had a hollow middle covered with delicate pink crystals that glimmered in the light. Emma thought it was the prettiest thing she'd ever seen.

"Go on! Try it out," said Sophy, nodding her head to the little star wolf.

Emma felt excitement tingling in her stomach.

She knelt down next to the wolf pup, holding the hollow stone tightly. She could hardly believe she was about to speak with a magical animal for the very first time!

Chapter Four

✦ ∶ ✹

The Unwelcome Visitors

Emma didn't want to scare the little wolf pup, so she spoke very softly. "Hello, I'm Emma. This magic stone will let us talk to each other. Do you understand me?"

The star wolf's eyes brightened. "Yes, I do!" he barked. "You got me out of that nasty trap. Thank you!"

"That's all right!" Emma smiled. "Do you have a name?"

"I'm called Teo!" The star wolf put his front paws on her knees. His tail wagged joyfully.

"Isn't there a star named Teo?" said Emma.

"Yes, there is! It's the first star to come out after sunset," explained the baby wolf. "And I was born one evening at the moment it appeared."

"How lovely to be named after a star," said Emma. "But how did you get stuck by yourself in that horrible trap?"

"I was looking for jem berries to eat," said the pup sadly. "I must have gone farther away from the pack than I thought. Then people came along and I heard my family dashing away!"

Emma stroked his thick fur. "Don't worry! As soon as your pack starts singing this evening we'll be able to find them and take you home."

"Why don't we have that treacle pudding," said Sophy. "Then we'll all feel a bit better!"

Sophy fetched bowls while Emma made warm custard to go with the pudding. They sat down to eat the delicious treat. Teo munched his helping eagerly and then licked every last bit from the bowl with his little pink tongue.

When they'd finished, Sophy showed Emma how to tie some thread around the two halves of her stone and make it into a loop. That way she could wear the stone around her neck, tucked under her clothes, where it couldn't be seen.

Sophy washed the dishes while Emma rolled out the pastry for the fruit pie. Teo explored each room of the treetop house. He became very fond of one fluffy yellow cushion. After carrying it all round the house, he made up a game where he took a running leap to land on top of it, sending it skidding along the floor.

"I never thought a wolf pup would love a cushion so much!" said Emma.

Teo wagged his tail as he ran to the corner to begin another running leap. "This is great fun!"

"Just be careful not to hurt yourself," Emma said, laughing.

Sophy put the last dish back in the cupboard. "There, that's all done!"

"Brilliant! And the pie is ready to go in the oven too." Emma bent down to open the oven, but stopped when she heard someone banging on the door.

"Who's that?" hissed Sophy.

"I don't know!" Emma peered round the edge of the curtain. "There's a man wearing rich clothes and—oh no!" She drew back quickly.

"What is it?" Sophy's eyes widened.

"It's the people that chased me in the forest—the trappers!" gasped Emma. "They must have come to take Teo away. We can't let them do that!"

"Let's hide him," said Sophy. "Teo, where are you?"

The little pup stopped sliding on the cushion and wagged his tail.

"You've got to stay really quiet." Emma picked him up and dashed to her bedroom. "Stay under the bed for a few minutes, okay?"

Teo licked her cheek and scampered right underneath. "I'll be very quiet!"

"Good boy!" whispered Emma, then she jumped as the trappers hammered on the door again.

"Maybe you should hide too," said Sophy. "What if they recognize you?"

"They only saw me from the back." Emma grabbed a hair band, tied up her light-brown hair, and tucked it under a straw hat. Then she pulled off her dark-blue cloak and stuffed it under the sofa. Hopefully they wouldn't realize that she was the same person they chased!

"I know someone's in there. Open up immediately!" said a man with a harsh voice. "This is Lord Hector, Defender of the Western Realm, appointed by order of Queen Viola."

Emma gulped. Then, trying to look calm, she opened the door. "Good afternoon, sir. Can I help you?"

A barrel-shaped man towered over her, glaring down with cold gray eyes. Emma knew he must be Lord Hector. He was wearing a smart black cloak and a red waistcoat. Behind him were the people who had chased after her that morning.

"You took a very long time opening the door," snapped Lord Hector. "Why?"

"I—I was cooking, sir!" Emma told him.

"I do NOT like to be kept waiting!" replied Lord Hector. "Don't you know who I am?"

Emma wasn't sure what to say to that.

"You're Lord Hector," Sophy said quickly. "You told us when you knocked on the door."

"I hope you're not trying to be funny!" Lord Hector scowled. "I am here on the instructions of Sir Fitzroy, who speaks on behalf of the queen. Magical creatures are no longer allowed to roam free in the Kingdom of Arramia."

"But that's not fair!" began Sophy.

"Don't be silly, girl," scoffed the nobleman. "It's not about being fair. It's about what's best. Someone from this dratted forest took a star wolf from my trap. So I'm checking every house in the village. I'll find the thief and punish them, that's for sure. It had better not be one of you two!" Behind him, his servants grinned nastily.

Emma didn't want to lie, but she wasn't going to give Teo away either. "Sorry! I can't help you at all!" she said at last.

"I can't either." Sophy put on a sad face. "We're really sorry!"

Lord Hector turned to the trappers behind him. "Simpson! Is one of these girls the thief you chased in the woods?"

The man peered at the girls. "Nah! It was someone a lot taller."

"Colby? What do you think?" said Lord Hector.

"I don't think so," said the woman. "But to be certain we should check their cloaks." She smirked and held up a scrap of dark-blue cloth. "If one of them has a blue cloak with a rip in it, we'll make them tell us exactly where the star wolf is."

Chapter Five

* .:*

Bravery and Baking

Emma choked back a gasp. She recognized the scrap of cloth held by Lord Hector's servant straightaway. It was exactly the same color as her cloak. It must have gotten left behind on the brambles as she ran to escape.

The woman, Colby, pushed forward. "We should search the place. They could be hiding the cloak with the rip in it." She stared at a stray wisp of hair hanging below Emma's straw hat.

"Don't let them in! I'm scared," came a tiny wolf cry from Emma's bedroom.

Emma's heart sank, but she reminded herself that only she and Sophy could understand what Teo had just said.

"What was that noise? Was it a cat?" Lord Hector frowned suspiciously.

"That was the baby," said Emma, thinking very quickly. "And I'm afraid you can't come in because you'd disturb him. He's just beginning his nap."

"It didn't sound like a child to me," said Simpson.

Teo let out another whine.

"I'm sorry! He's getting upset. He probably needs his bottle. Good-bye!" Emma closed the door firmly and shut Lord Hector out.

Sophy stared at her. "Emma, you were amazing!"

"Thanks!" Emma pulled off the straw hat. She leaned against the closed door, her heart thumping. She was afraid that Lord Hector would bang on the door again and demand to be let in, but when she peeked round the curtain she saw him pointing to the other treetop houses. His servants were talking and nodding.

Lord Hector took a tiny glass bottle from his waistcoat pocket. Blue liquid glistened inside as he lifted it to the light.

"What are they saying?" whispered Sophy.

Emma leaned closer to the window, still

keeping out of sight. She could only hear snip-
pets of their conversation.

"Someone must be hiding the silly creature," said Simpson. "We'll keep searching for
you, my lord."

"Then we'll grab the little beast!" added Colby.

"Bring the wolf straight to me," Lord Hector
ordered them. "I have a plan!" He smiled and
handed the little bottle to Simpson. "And keep
this safe—we'll need it later."

Emma drew back from the window once
they'd gone. She shivered. "We have to get Teo
out of here without them seeing. He's in terrible danger!"

"They're bad people!" said Sophy. "Magical
animals are special and beautiful, but they just
can't see that. I think deep down they're afraid
of magic!"

Emma nodded. "Let's stick to our plan and sneak out when the sun sets. Then we can track down the star wolves when they start to sing." She hurried to the bedroom. "Teo, it's all right! The horrid people are gone."

There was no sound from the little pup.

Emma crouched down and peered under the bed. "Teo?"

The little star wolf was curled up on his side, his eyes shut tight. Emma gently put a blanket over him to keep him warm. Then she tiptoed out of the room, putting a finger to her lips to let Sophy know she should stay quiet.

"Well, it has been a very tiring day!" whispered Sophy as Emma closed

the bedroom door. "What shall we do? It must be hours till sunset."

Emma put on the oven gloves and placed the fruit pie in the oven. "We need to make more of these for the market. We'll also need cakes, buns, and doughnuts." She ticked each one off on her fingers. "If we bake enough we can take some

with us tonight. We don't want to get hungry!"

"Sometimes Cook lets me help with the baking at the castle," said Sophy. "But I've never made doughnuts before!"

"I'll show you how to do it!" Emma fetched them both aprons and showed Sophy how to make the dough.

The kitchen filled with delicious smells. White flour got sprinkled all over the worktop. The girls' fingers became sticky with butter and jem berry jam. They worked hard, mixing and measuring. Plates full of freshly baked cakes were soon stacked on the side to cool.

"These smell gorgeous!" said Sophy, admiring the finished doughnuts.

"Let's try one before we pack the rest up for the market." Emma bit into a doughnut. "Mm, I think they're the best ones I've ever made."

Sophy ate one too and then looked longingly at the other doughnuts. "Shame we can't have another one!"

"I know, but we need them for the stall!" said Emma, smiling.

The girls packed up the cakes and other goodies they'd baked. Emma hurried down to the market and gave everything to her parents, while Sophy stayed in the treetop house in case Teo woke up. Emma's mom and dad thanked her for baking so much. Their stall was already crowded with customers.

By the time Emma walked home, the sun was sinking in the sky. When it grew darker, the lanterns would be lit and the festival would begin. Already the musicians were practicing their tunes.

There had been no sign of Lord Hector or

his servants at the market, but this only made Emma more nervous. She was sure they hadn't given up on catching Teo, so where were they? She looked around carefully before going back inside her house.

The little wolf pup leapt on her as soon as she opened the front door. "Emma, you're back!" he yelped.

"Teo! You made me jump," laughed Emma. Kneeling down, she hugged him and buried her face in his thick fur.

"He woke up while you were out," explained Sophy. "I think he misses the other star wolves."

Teo jumped onto an armchair near the window and said wistfully, "Soon my pack will gather round to sing the Sky Song. I don't know if I can sing it the right way by myself."

"You don't have to!" Emma joined him by the window. "We're going to take you back to your family. Let's pack up ready to go."

Emma and Sophy filled a backpack with bread rolls, slices of fruit pie, and a thermos of water. Emma found an old purple cloak in her wardrobe. It was a little short, but she didn't dare to wear the torn blue one in case someone noticed.

"I'll hide you under here until we've left

Tangleberry Rise," she told Teo, folding her cloak over him.

They crept along the treetop bridges. The sun had set, leaving a golden smudge on the horizon. The branches of the trees looked black against the deep-blue sky. Lots of people were walking toward the clearing, ready for the start of the festival. The band began to play a cheerful tune.

Emma loved the Lantern Festival, but today all that mattered was getting Teo back to his family. Silently, she and Sophy climbed down to the ground and slipped away between the trees.

Chapter Six

✦ ∴ ✹

The Sky Song

Emma tiptoed out of Tangleberry Rise with Sophy close behind her. She held the wolf pup tightly, stroking his fur when he started to wriggle. The forest was growing darker with every minute. Overhanging leaves brushed against their hair. The cawing of a raven echoed down from the branches above.

"Emma!" Sophy whispered, pointing through the trees.

Two figures were standing right in the middle of the path. The taller figure was Simpson. He was holding up a lamp with a grumpy look on his face.

"It's Lord Hector's servants," said Emma. "They must be watching to see who leaves the village. But where's Lord Hector?"

"Probably eating his dinner while they do the hard work," murmured Sophy. "How do we get away without them seeing us?"

"I know a secret way," whispered Emma. "Follow me!"

Hurrying back up to the treetop walkway,

they crossed a narrow rope bridge leading to a broad oak tree. Looking down, Emma could barely see the ground in the darkness. The wind swirled, making the leaves whisper as if the trees were tell-
ing secrets to one another.

"Be careful!" warned Emma. "I've never done this in the dark before."

"Don't worry," Sophy whispered back. "I'm a good climber."

Carefully, Emma clambered down the oak's sturdy branches and waited for Sophy at the bottom. Then they scrambled down a steep bank and dashed along a dried-up riverbed with tall earth walls on either side. This was Emma's secret way out of Tangleberry Rise. Down here at the bottom of the ditch, no one could see them.

They followed the dried-up riverbed for a long time before climbing up the banks again. The village was far behind and the sounds of the Lantern Festival could barely be heard beneath the swishing of the leaves.

"Teo, are you all right?" asked Emma, drawing back her cloak.

"Yes!" Teo's eyes brightened and he raised his nose to sniff the air. "The song will begin soon!"

"Do you know where your pack might go to sing it?" said Sophy.

Teo tilted his head thoughtfully. "Sometimes they go to Star Rock. You can see the sky from there."

"Star Rock?" Emma wrinkled her forehead. "I don't know that place."

"I'll show you!" Teo leapt out of her arms and scampered away.

"Teo, wait!" Sophy called after him. "What if Lord Hector's servants have set more traps? You could run straight into one."

Teo dashed back to Sophy, his tail wagging. "I'll go slowly if you like!"

"Good boy!" Sophy patted the wolf pup. "It's very dark now. Maybe we should have brought a lamp."

"Don't worry! The Whispering Forest has its

own lights." Emma grinned as she saw Sophy's puzzled face. "Wait and see!"

As they walked on, tiny dots of light began appearing on the trees and bushes. They shone in many different colors, from buttercup yellow to deep purple. The lights grew brighter and larger, and each one looked transparent, as if the light was captured inside a glass.

"What are they?" Sophy looked around in amazement.

"Crystal glow worms!" Emma told her. "They're beautiful, aren't they? Now we shan't need a lamp at all."

The forest sparkled with the glow worms' colorful lights. Emma beamed as she gazed around. It looked like a magical wonderland.

Teo bounded up to one of the tiny creatures and sniffed it. The glow worm's light went out.

"Teo!" Emma laughed. "Leave it alone!"

"Oops, sorry!" Teo scampered away and the glow worm's light blinked back on.

Emma pointed out nocturnal forest animals to Sophy: bat-wing moths with their velvety black wings and field mice with long whiskers. They even spotted a large feathery shape at the top of a tree with pale-yellow eyes and sharp talons. The glittering white feathers on its tummy were a diamond shape.

"That's a diamond owl," whispered Emma. "They're not always very friendly."

The diamond owl spread its enormous wings and gave a piercing squawk before flying away.

"Are diamond owls magical?" said Sophy, gazing after it.

"There are stories about their speed and magical eyesight, but I've never been close enough to one to see for myself." Emma broke off, distracted by Teo's calls.

"I thought they'd be here!" cried the wolf pup. "Why aren't they here?"

Emma ran to catch up with him. The little star wolf was standing on the edge of a clearing with a tall pointed rock in the center. Emma could imagine the star wolves circling the rock and lifting their heads to the sky to sing.

"Where have they gone?" The pup's voice wobbled.

Emma hugged him tightly. "We'll find them—you'll see! As soon as they start to sing we'll be able to follow the sound."

Sophy climbed onto a flat ledge halfway up the rock. "The sky looks so black without the stars."

Emma climbed up beside her, and Teo sprang onto her lap. "I'm sure it won't be long now," she said. "Do you ever hear the star wolves at the castle, Sophy?"

"No," said Sophy. "We're much too far away. But I've heard stories about them and I've always wished—" She stopped and turned her head. "Can you hear something?"

Teo's ears pricked up. "The Sky Song is beginning!"

The voices of the star wolves rose in a gentle melody. It started softly then grew stronger, with different notes weaving in and out of the song. Emma had heard the music many times, but she'd never been able to understand the words before. She held her breath, listening.

"Teo!" The star wolves repeated the same word. "Teee-o!" They sang it softly at first. Then the music became a string of quick running notes. At last they chanted it forcefully, as if telling someone to wake up.

"Teo—that's the name of the first star," whispered Emma. "They're calling to it."

"Teo!" The wolf pup wagged his tail. "It's my name too!"

A bright-yellow star lit up in the middle of the dark sky. It beamed down on the forest, shining a little brighter every time the star wolves sang its name.

"Wow!" breathed Sophy. "They called to it and it appeared!"

Emma's heart skipped a beat. It was so amazing being able to understand what the star wolves were singing. She shook herself out of her daydream and scrambled down the rock. "We shouldn't be standing here!" she called to

Sophy. "We have to find the star wolves before they stop singing and disappear into the forest. We'd better hurry!"

Chapter Seven

Lord Hector's Wicked Plan

Emma led the way. She dodged round trees and leapt over bushes. Every few minutes she stopped to check she was following the sound of the singing. The magical wolves had begun calling to a star called Silva. After Silva, they sang to Kaya and then to Pollus.

Glancing upward, Emma saw there were now four bright stars in the night sky. How many more stars would the wolves call with their song? What if she couldn't reach them in time?

Teo bounded past. "This way! Not far now."

"Are you sure you know where you're going, Teo?" said Emma.

"Yes, yes! Follow me!" The pup galloped away, his tail wagging.

"The song seems louder," said Sophy breathlessly. "We must be getting close."

The girls and the wolf pup ran down a hill into a small wooded valley. On the top of the next rise, they could see a crowd of silvery-gray wolves with their heads lifted to the sky. Each wolf had a star shape on its forehead that glowed softly in the darkness.

"The star wolves!" said Emma. "Well done, Teo! You took us straight to them."

Teo raised his furry nose in the air and joined in with the music. His little voice was high and clear. Some of the wolves turned at the sound of his singing and their tails waved in delight.

Two figures moved in the shadow of the trees. Their lamp wasn't lit and they were hard to see in the darkness. They sneaked out of their hiding place and crept toward the star wolves.

Emma spotted them. "Oh no! It's Lord Hector's servants. They must have followed the wolves' song like we did."

"Teo, wait!" hissed Sophy. "It's not safe!"

The wolf pup didn't hear

68

Sophy's call. He was halfway up the hill and getting closer to the place where Lord Hector's
servants were lurking.

The star wolves went on singing and another
star appeared, glittering with silvery light.

Emma dashed up the slope. Her legs pumped
quickly. Her heart thudded in her chest. "Teo!"
she gasped. "Wait!"

Colby darted forward, grabbed hold of Teo,
and stuffed him under her arm. The wolf pup
gave a terrified whimper.

"Sophy! Help me get Teo back," cried Emma.

Sophy sprinted up the hill. "I'm right behind
you!"

Emma ran fast. Her eyes were fixed on Teo,
struggling in Colby's arms. There was a snap as her
foot hit the ground and something closed around
her ankle. She lost her balance and fell over.

"Emma!" cried Sophy. "Are you all right?"

"Ouch! Something hurt me." Emma checked her ankle and found a wooden cage around her foot. "It's one of those traps. The servants must have set more of them."

"You opened one before, didn't you?" Sophy crouched down next to her. "I'll help you."

"Quickly!" gasped Emma. "I don't think the trappers have noticed us yet."

Farther up the hill, Simpson struck a match to light his lamp. "Perfect!" he boomed, making no effort to keep his voice down. "We only need one beast to do this experiment. Hold it still and I'll give it the special liquid."

Teo began to wriggle and cry. Colby shook him lightly. "Stop that!"

"This will make him quiet." Simpson pulled out a tiny glass bottle filled with blue liquid.

70

"Lord Hector bought this special stuff on the journey. He says it'll take away the creatures' voices. If it works, there'll be no squeaking and yapping from this little beast ever again!"

"Why are we only giving it to one of them?" said Colby, rubbing her forehead. "There's a whole pack of wolves on that hill. Don't you think we should give it to all of them?"

"We're checking if it works first, silly! Then we'll make the rest of them drink it too. Their squealing noise is supposed to be magical," sneered Simpson. "Well, it won't be for much longer!"

Emma covered her mouth with her hand. She was glad that Teo couldn't understand what the servants were saying.

Hearing Teo's whine, the star wolves broke off their song and bounded down the hillside toward the little pup.

"Colby! The beasts are coming!" Simpson dropped his lamp as he started to run. The light smashed and the burning candle lay on the ground. Without stopping to look back, Lord Hector's servants ran away through the trees, taking Teo with them.

Emma struggled with the fastening on the trap. Sophy leaned over, trying to help. The candle flame spread, burning the twigs and dead leaves on the ground. A tiny fire began to grow.

"Danger!" yelped the star wolves. "Fire in the forest!"

Sophy jiggled the catch on the trap and the wooden door sprang open.

Emma lifted her foot free. "Thanks, Sophy! We have to stop that fire. Quick, where's our water?" She delved into their backpack for the thermos, before dashing up the hill.

The fire fizzled out as soon as Emma poured water onto the flames. Gray smoke drifted away into the air.

"That was good thinking," Sophy told her.

"Thanks." Emma scanned the trees close by. "We have to find Teo. Did you see which way Lord Hector's servants went?"

"This way, I think." Sophy raced into a thicket at the bottom of the hill. "Come on! We can still catch them."

Together, they ran through the forest. Leaves rustled not far ahead. They followed the noise, realizing too late that it was only a swift hare running up and down the trunk of a tree.

"What do we do now?" said Sophy. "They could be anywhere!"

Emma bit her lip. "We should head back to Tangleberry Rise. That's where Lord Hector will be waiting."

"But they've got a head start!" Sophy's eyes filled with tears. "You heard what they said. They've got that potion…" She trailed off.

Emma's stomach turned over at the thought of that little bottle filled with blue potion. Could it really take a creature's voice away? What if Teo wasn't able to sing anymore? What if he couldn't speak to anyone? He would feel so sad.

A huge pale bird swooped down and landed

in a nearby tree. The branches swayed under its weight.

Glancing up, Emma saw the pale-yellow eyes of a diamond owl glaring down at her. "Hello! Can you help us?" she yelled, but the owl didn't answer. Desperately, she flung the backpack on the ground and started climbing the tree.

"Emma! What are you doing?" asked Sophy.

"I'm going to talk to the owl," Emma called back. "We need help from the biggest, cleverest, most magical creature we can find."

Chapter Eight

Owl Power

Emma pulled herself up the tree. She was glad the branches were strong and the light from the crystal glow worms made it easy to see. Her heart thumped as she looked down. The ground was now a long way away. Fixing her eyes on the tree trunk, she kept on climbing.

"I'm right behind you!" called Sophy, climbing up too.

The branches at the top quivered. The diamond owl was taller than a man. He stared down, his pale-yellow eyes never blinking. On his chest was a diamond-shaped patch of glittering white feathers.

Just as Emma reached the branch below the owl, the gigantic bird spread his wings to fly away. "Oh, please wait!" cried Emma, holding on to the tree trunk to steady herself. "There's a little star wolf in danger and we could save him if you'd only help us. Please, we really need you!"

The diamond owl folded his wings, saying sternly. "What is this? How can you—a human— speak like a diamond owl?"

"Oh! I should have explained. We have special stones that let us speak to all magical animals," said Emma.

The owl ruffled his feathers disapprovingly. "Humans! You're always meddling in things you don't understand."

"We're not trying to meddle!" Sophy climbed up beside her friend. "We're just helping the star wolves."

"Raak! Naughty girl!" The owl pecked angrily at the tree trunk, making the branches wobble. "YOU must be the reason we only have five stars out tonight. Just look at the sky!"

Emma peered upward. The diamond owl was right. Only five stars shone in the darkness. Usually there were dozens. The sky looked wrong without them.

"That wasn't our fault at all. Please, just listen

for a moment," begged Emma. "The only thing that matters right now is Teo." Talking quickly, she told the owl all about the traps in the forest and how the servants were taking the wolf pup back to Lord Hector right now.

The diamond owl shifted and his white feathers shimmered. When Emma finished, the creature gazed at her for a moment without speaking. His yellow eyes looked like lanterns in the darkness. "You have some goodness in you, even though you're human," the owl said at last. "You may call me Kellan."

"So you'll help us?" asked Sophy.

"There isn't much time," Emma added nervously.

"It is lucky for your friend the wolf pup that we diamond owls have magical eyes that can see right through things—branches, tree trunks,

anything! We also have the speed of the wind."
Kellan blinked slowly and the white feathers on
his chest glittered. "Climb on, before I change
my mind."

"Thank you!" said Emma. "We think the bad-
dies were heading back to Tangleberry Rise."

"Then you are right," said Kellan. "There's no
time to lose. Come fly with me!"

The girls scrambled onto the diamond owl's
back and held tight to his pale feathers. Kellan
spread his wings and soared into the sky. He
circled over the treetops and then sped up,
so that everything became a blur.

"Wow!" shouted Sophy. "I've never gone as
fast as this on Windrunner's back."

Emma felt dizzy and the wind roared in her
ears. She held on tightly, telling herself that if
they found Teo it would all be worth it.

"I see them!" squawked Kellan, diving into the trees.

Branches snapped as they plunged downward. Twigs snagged in Emma's hair and leaves scattered in all directions.

"What are you going to do?" Emma shouted to the owl.

"I shall spook them!" replied Kellan. "They won't know what's happening!"

The diamond owl swooped through the trees with Emma and Sophy on his back. Just ahead, two figures had nearly reached the main path that led to Tangleberry Rise.

"Wooo-hoo!" The diamond owl swept past, hooting into the servants' ears.

Simpson and Colby swung round, but the owl had already soared into the treetops.

"Emma! Sophy! Where are you?" The pup's sad whimper echoed through the trees.

"That's Teo!" Emma's heart ached. "He sounds so frightened."

"Not as frightened as the humans will be." Kellan swooped down again, hooting even louder into the servants' ears.

"Help! It's a ghost," shrieked Colby.

"It's a monster!" shouted Simpson.

In their hurry to get away, they tripped each

other up and fell over. Colby let go of Teo, who scampered away into a bush.

Simpson stumbled to his feet, his voice squeaky with fear. "Run! The monsters are attacking!"

"Raaak!" Kellan glided past a third time, delivering an earsplitting squawk over Colby's head.

"Wait for me!" Colby gasped as she fled.

The diamond owl flew gently to the ground and allowed the girls to climb down from his back. "Silly humans!" He folded his wings and glared at the disappearing servants. "They probably don't even know what a diamond owl is."

"Well, I do! You're the most amazing bird I've ever met!" Emma threw herself against Kellan, pressing her cheek into his glittering white feathers. "Thanks so much for helping us."

"Well, well!" The owl ruffled his feathers as if he wasn't sure whether to like being hugged or not. "It's quite all right! Now, where's that wolf pup?"

Emma spotted a silver-gray shape behind a bush. "Teo? It's all right. You're safe now."

Teo peered out, his black eyes still fearful. As soon as he saw Emma, he bounded into her arms and licked her face with his little pink tongue.

"Teo!" Emma laughed. "We found you!"

"You've been really brave." Sophy scratched the pup between his ears.

"I'm so glad you came!" Teo gave Sophy a lick on the cheek too.

Kellan studied the pup with narrowed eyes. "Well, the creature is furry enough, if you like that sort of thing. And he certainly has a wet tongue."

Emma giggled. "Teo, this is Kellan. We couldn't have found you without his help." She turned to the owl. "Would you help us with one more thing? Lord Hector's servants left some animal traps around the forest. We need to find them all before they hurt any more creatures."

Kellan bowed. "It would be my pleasure! Climb on, fair humans and small furry thing. We shall find these nasty traps and break them to smithereens!"

Chapter Nine

★ ⋅∘⋆

The Tiny Potion Bottle

Emma, Sophy, and Teo climbed onto the diamond owl's back. Emma held on to Teo with one hand and to Kellan's feathers with the other. The diamond owl glided over the treetops, using his magical eyes to spot the wooden traps. As soon as he caught sight of one, he dived through the trees to the ground.

Many of the traps were broken with a swift peck from Kellan's beak. Some of them were smashed by Emma and Sophy using large sticks. Teo joined in by growling fiercely every time they found one.

After they had broken twelve traps, Kellan circled over the whole forest. "I believe we've uncovered them all," he told them. "Our job is done."

"Thank you so much," said Emma. "We should take Teo back to the star wolves."

"I saw them gathered by Star Rock." Kellan wheeled round and zoomed over the trees.

At last Emma gazed down and spotted the clearing with the tall gray rock. A crowd of silvery wolves circled the base of Star Rock, their heads tilted to the sky. The diamond owl glided to the ground and Emma, Sophy, and Teo slid smoothly from his back.

"I shall go now," said Kellan. "But if you ever need me again, use the call of the diamond owls. Too-hoo raak!"

"Thank you—we will!" called Emma as the huge owl flew into the night sky.

"Baby Teo!" One of the star wolves leapt forward to greet the pup.

"Mommy!" Teo nuzzled his mother's fur. "I missed you!"

"I was so worried when we couldn't find you," said his mother. "We saw traps among the trees. Then those bad people took you away and started the fire. Are you sure you're all right?"

"I'm fine, Mommy!" yelped Teo. "These girls

rescued me and
they can talk to us
because they have
magic Speaking
Stones."

The star wolves
gathered round Emma and Sophy. They had
beautiful silvery fur and deep black eyes just like
Teo's. The markings on their coats gleamed in
the starlight.

"Our little pup has returned!" said one.

"Can these girls really speak to us?" asked
another.

"Yes, what Teo said is true! This is the special stone that lets me talk to all of you." Emma
showed them her hollow stone lined with delicate pink crystals. "And you don't need to worry
about the traps. The diamond owl helped us

find every single one. Now they're all broken."

"Then the danger is over!" said Teo's mother. "How can I ever thank you enough for helping Teo? You've done so much!"

Teo leapt into Emma's arms. "And now we're best friends!"

Emma laughed and hugged the little pup. "You're so sweet!"

"Will you stay and hear us sing?" asked Teo's mother. "We didn't finish our Sky Song this evening. If we don't finish it soon, the other stars will stay hidden and the sky will be dark."

Emma glanced upward. There were still only five stars shining and the faint starlight hardly brightened the darkness at all. She exchanged looks with Sophy. "Lord Hector's still out there," she said quietly to her friend. "And his servants still have that little bottle of blue potion."

Sophy nodded. "You're right. We should go back."

Emma turned to the star wolves. "We'd love to stay and listen to the Sky Song, but there's one more thing we have to do."

Teo's mother nodded her shaggy head. "Then promise you will visit us as soon as you can. I should like to know you better!"

"And then you can play with me!" said Teo, his tail wagging.

"We'd love to visit!" said Emma.

As they left the clearing, the girls heard the star wolves begin their song. The beautiful melody echoed through the trees. There was something in the music that made Emma's heart beat faster—as if the song was happy and sad all at the same time.

As they drew closer to Tangleberry Rise, the song of the star wolves was drowned out by

the noise coming from the village. There were drums thumping and guitars twanging, as well as shouts of laughter.

"How are we going to get hold of that potion bottle?" said Sophy.

"I don't know." Emma stopped to catch her breath. "I just know we have to. Those servants said the potion could take away a star wolf's voice. What would they do if they couldn't sing?"

The girls hurried toward the center of Tangleberry Rise where the festival was in full swing. The party was being held in a clearing beneath the treetop houses. Golden lanterns hung on every branch, filling the place with light. The band was playing and lots of people were dancing.

A crowded outdoor café was serving soup, rolls, and jem berry cakes. Emma caught a glimpse of her parents selling the fruit pies and doughnuts she'd made that afternoon. Everyone was talking and laughing and enjoying themselves.

All except Lord Hector.

The rich nobleman was sitting with his arms folded and a deep frown on his face. A sugar-coated doughnut and a cup of juice lay on the table in front of him. He hadn't taken a single bite of the doughnut. Colby and Simpson sat beside him. Colby was chewing her nails nervously.

"I wonder if Simpson still has the bottle of potion," whispered Sophy.

"One of them must have it." Emma edged closer. "We have to get rid of it, otherwise the star wolves will never be safe." She swallowed. Lord Hector had such a mean look on his face. How was she going to get that potion bottle without being seen?

Chapter Ten

* . *

The Lantern Festival

Emma and Sophy tiptoed over to the café and crouched behind a table close to where Lord Hector was sitting.

"So we really couldn't fight all those wild animals in the dark," Simpson was saying. "There were so many of them screeching at us!"

"You caught one wolf pup and you managed to lose it again!" growled Lord Hector, drinking up the last of his juice. "I've never met any servants more hopeless than you!"

"But when daylight comes we can go back and—" Colby broke off as Lord Hector slammed his cup down on the table.

"ENOUGH OF THE EXCUSES!" Lord Hector yelled so loudly that people turned round to stare.

"Sorry, My Lord! I'll get you another drink," stammered Colby, hurrying away.

"Now, give me back that potion," Lord Hector told Simpson. "I don't trust you to look after it anymore. The woman who sold it to me said it can never be replaced because the recipe has been lost. I don't want you spoiling everything."

"Yes, My Lord." Simpson got out the little glass bottle and put it on the table.

Emma and Sophy crept closer and hid behind a chair. They were almost close enough to touch Lord Hector!

"We just need to wait until they're not looking," Emma whispered into Sophy's ear.

Colby came back and placed a jug of blackcurrant juice on the table. The band struck up another tune and lots of people began to dance.

Lord Hector glared round. "I hate these silly people with their ridiculous festival!"

Simpson and Colby turned to stare at the people dancing. While they were all looking the other way, Emma dashed forward and reached for the potion. The bottle toppled over and the lid fell off. Heart thumping, Emma grabbed the bottle before it rolled across the table.

As she took it away, a single drop of blue liquid fell from the bottle and landed in the jug of blackcurrant juice. Emma darted back to her hiding place and handed the potion bottle to Sophy. "Some fell in the juice!" she said breathlessly. "I must go back and take that jug away."

"It's too late!" whispered Sophy. "Look!"

Simpson had turned back and poured juice into all three cups. The girls held their breath as Lord Hector and his servants drank the juice.

"Maybe the potion won't work," said Sophy. "It was only one drop."

The band finished playing their tune and, in the moment of quiet, notes of the wolves' song drifted over the trees.

"When I get hold of those wolves, the first thing I'm going to do is stop their stupid singing," snarled Lord Hector. "Colby, why does this juice taste so strange?" He took another sip from his cup.

"It's blackcurrant, My Lord." Colby drank some and frowned.

"Ugh! That tastes disgusting." Lord Hector drained his cup. "Now, where's that potion bottle? Simpson, where did you put it?"

Simpson looked puzzled. "I left it right here on the table!"

"Where is it, then?" croaked Lord Hector. "And

99

why am I losing my voice? What have you done, you stupid—" He broke off and started coughing.

Simpson and Colby were croaking too. From their pointing it was clear that they were blaming each other.

Lord Hector turned bright red. Shaking his fist, he chased his servants out of the clearing.

Emma giggled. "Did you see Lord Hector's face?"

"He was furious!" said Sophy. "I'm not sorry they've lost their voices for a while. They weren't saying very nice things anyway!"

Emma's dad came over wearing a stripy apron over his clothes. "There you are, Emma! We've nearly sold out of the things you baked. Maybe you and your friend would like a jem berry cake before they're all gone."

"Yes, please!" said Emma. "Are you hungry, Sophy?"

"Really hungry!" Sophy nodded.

Emma glanced upward as she followed her dad to their stall. The sky was full of stars from east to west and north to south. They were scattered across the darkness like glittering diamonds.

The band finished another tune. In the sudden silence, the final notes of the star wolves' song floated through the trees.

Emma and Sophy had a wonderful time at the Lantern Festival. They bobbed for apples and joined in with a game of freeze tag. The band went on playing till late and the girls danced and danced until their feet ached.

Emma's mom and dad invited Sophy to stay at their house. They found it a little strange that a maid from the royal castle was so far from home but they accepted Sophy's explanation that she had important things to do in the forest.

The next day, the girls made a picnic and went out into the woods. Sophy was to meet Windrunner at midday in the clearing near the jem berry bushes. It was a beautiful morning and the girls stopped now and then to pick berries to eat. Rabbits and squirrels scurried among the fallen leaves, while emerald woodpeckers tapped against the tree trunks. A playful breeze swirled through the forest, making the leaves whisper.

The girls spread their picnic blanket under an enormous red-and-white toadstool. They ate sandwiches and thick slices of strawberry cake while watching the giant silverwing butterflies flutter from flower to flower.

"I've had such an amazing time," sighed Sophy as they packed the picnic away. "I really don't want to go, but I know

there's so much more to be done. Other magical animals could be in danger too."

"I'd like to come and help with the secret rescues one day," said Emma. "I could fly on Kellan, the diamond owl."

Sophy hugged her. "Thanks, Emma!"

The sound of wingbeats filled the air and Windrunner appeared, soaring over the tree-tops. The wind buffeted the trees as he landed.

"Greetings, Sophy! I'm glad to see you're both safe and well," he said in his deep growly voice.

"Windrunner! We've had such an exciting time." Sophy climbed on to the dragon's bumpy back. "I'll tell you all about it. Good-bye, Emma! Thanks for having me to stay."

"Bye, Sophy! Bye, Windrunner!" Emma waved as Sophy sailed into the air on the enormous storm dragon.

Sophy and Windrunner disappeared above the trees. Emma turned away, feeling a little sad that all the excitement was over. Leaves rustled nearby and a little pair of dark eyes peeked out from behind a tree trunk.

"Teo?" said Emma. "Is that you?"

The little wolf pup leapt out of his hiding place and bounded over to greet her. "Emma, we found you!"

A taller star wolf followed Teo into the clearing. Teo's mother bowed her head. "We followed the sound of your voice. I wanted to thank you again for helping Teo."

"That's all right!" Emma bowed her head to Teo's mother before kneeling down to hug the baby star wolf.

"All the forest creatures know about your brave actions, from the largest diamond owl right down to the tiniest mouse," said Teo's mother. "And the star wolves have made up a new song in your honor."

"Come and hear it now!" begged Teo. "Oh, please!"

"I'd love to!" Emma let them lead her through the trees.

The star wolves were gathered in a circle and Emma sat down among them, hugging her knees. Their music began softly but then it grew louder. Emma smiled as the song described how she'd rescued Teo and taken him flying through the air on the back of a diamond owl.

She touched her magical stone as she listened to the beautiful melody. She'd never thought she would be lucky enough to become friends with the magical animals. It was like a dream come true!